Herman the Great

by ZORA LOUISE OLSEN

Illustrated by BARBARA COONEY

SCHOLASTIC INC.
New York Toronto London Auckland Sydney

So many helped —

Especially the real Marc and Herman
who really lived part of this story

To dearest Ernie, who never
stopped believing

To the sound of Lisa's
laughter in all the right places

To those special two —
Michele and Tim

To Ellen and her way
with animals

Not to forget John and my many other young friends
who first heard the story and kept asking for more!

ISBN 0-590-09807-1

12 11 10 9 8 7   5 6 7 8 9/8 0/9

Herman Chooses a Master

SOME say he was born with a super-brain. But truly, at the very beginning Herman was no different from most other white mice. He was born, one of a family of five, in the Pet Department of Woolworth's store in Hollywood — right next to the fish. He had the same tiny pink eyes, the same swirly pink tail as his brothers and sisters. Who could guess at the beginning that here was a mouse destined to make the whole wide world sit up and take note of all mousehood?

His very first memories were of a blur of bright colors as the fish swam past the cage containing himself, his mother, his brothers, and his sisters.

Next he became aware of faces — big people faces. Fat faces, pale faces, smiling faces, growling faces, sweet faces, mean faces. All staring. Staring at him. They stared if Herman wiggled his nose. They stared if he twitched his tail. Some stared with their mouths open. Some mouths had great big teeth in them — or lollipops. Living in a store can be rather spooky, you know.

Soon Herman became aware of something quite important. The faces not only stared, they also made noises — and *these funny noises meant something!*

At first Herman did not have the least idea what the sounds meant. But he listened. How he listened! All the time, while his brothers and sisters were chasing their tails, Herman listened to the people. And in just a few weeks he even knew what they were saying. Mostly they said the same things. One day he decided to make a survey. He titled it: "Things 100 People Said About Us."

> 30 people said, "Look at the mice."
> 20 said, "Mom, can I have a mouse? Mom, I want a mouse. Please let me have a mouse!"
> 20 said, "Oh, my word NO!"
> 8 said, "Aren't they cute?"
> 20 said, "I hate mice."
> 2 said, "Watch out! They bite!"

When Herman told his mother what the faces had said about their biting, she really got mad. "That is a lie!" she squeaked. "A lie! Maybe some do, but no one in our family bites. You just remember that, son!"

It was not long before Herman wanted to get away from Woolworth's. Somehow he knew that way out there, beyond the big plate-glass door, there must be Something Better. And he very much wanted Something Better!

One day Herman's big chance came. Into the store came a very nice boy, nine years old, with a most pleasant face. He told the pet clerk that his dream had always been to own a white mouse. He said he had saved up his own money to buy a mouse plus more money to buy the very best cage for his pet.

Suddenly Herman knew that's what he wanted too — the best. The Very Best! Herman very much wanted this boy to belong to him.

When the time came to choose his mouse, the boy bent down, looked in the cage, and saw most of the mice lying around on each other. But one mouse was standing up in the front of the cage, smiling and twitching his whiskers and acting Outstanding. You know who that one was, don't you? Herman. Of course.

The boy smiled, looked deep into this Outstanding mouse's pink eyes, and said, "Hello, Herman. My name is Marc."

Now nobody, *nobody* had ever called him by a name before. It had always been, "that mouse," or "this mouse," or "leave the mice alone." Suddenly Herman knew who he was. He was not just any old mouse. By golly, he was *Herman* — that's who he was. More than ever he wanted to belong to this kid named Marc. So when Marc put his finger into the cage, Herman remembered what his mother had told him. He did not bite. He just kind of nibbled. Ever so gently.

"That," said the boy, *"that* is *my* mouse!"

"And that," whispered Herman to himself, "*that* is *my* boy who said that!"

So the boy paid his money — 99¢ for Herman, $6.50 for the best steel cage and exercise wheel, 69¢ for sawdust, 85¢ for mice meal, and 43¢ for mouse vitamins. Herman felt a wild wave of excitement when he was put into the new cage. It was larger than the one he had shared with his mother, his sisters, and his brothers. He, Herman, had pulled off the deal! Then he heard the boy say to the clerk, "I'm going to send this mouse into (something that sounded like) *ow ter spay ss.*"

Herman didn't have the least idea what "ow ter spay ss" was, and he began to worry a bit. "Oh, well," he thought as the boy started to carry him in the cage, "at least it isn't Woolworth's."

Herman Faces the World

THE familiar fish had vanished. Even though Herman stood up eagerly and used his eyes, he could not see much of the world at first because he had to get used to something: *mo-shun*. That is spelled m-o-t-i-o-n but it sounds like *moshun*. Anyway if you have never experienced it, the first time you do, it can be a bit wild.

At first Herman saw only a fast whirr of bright and strange things. Of course he did not know what they were. To understand, put yourself in Herman's paws and imagine pots, plates, dolls, sink stoppers, earrings, gumdrops, lipstick, and hamburgers all flying past you.

As Herman clutched the bars of his cage for support, the first important truth about the world flashed in his mind like a brightly lit sign:

THE WORLD IS NOT ONLY FISH!

The world, he was finding out, is made up of a lot of things. And to a mouse it could be confusing!

In fact, after Herman's first trip to Marc's house, it took him two whole days to feel right again. His cage had been put in Marc's room. On one side of him was a model rocket, and on the other side lived a caterpillar in a jar.

At first Herman was very lonely. It was nice to have a bigger cage. But the caterpillar was not nearly as beautiful nor as interesting as the rainbow-colored fish that had swum past his cage at the store. Also, he missed his mother. And he missed his brothers and sisters too. In the store he had thought it would be so good — oh, boy how good it would be — to get away from his brothers and sisters climbing all over him and from his mother's squeaking all day long: "Herman, wash your tail. Herman, eat your grain. Herman, go run on the exercise wheel — it's good for you. Herman, stop staring at the fish — it's not polite. Herman, don't you *ever* bite, son."

Now all day long his boy was away most of the time at a place called *skool*. (That really is spelled s-c-h-o-o-l, as you well know, but remember, Herman had not learned how to spell.) There were no sounds to listen to. . . nobody to squeak to.

Have you ever seen a mouse cry?

Their tears are ever so tiny, and they are hard to see. Herman cried that first day at Marc's house. Then, because there was nobody to talk to, Herman talked to himself.

"Boy," he said, "are you silly, Herman. You are one silly mouse. You thought it would be such a good deal to leave Woolworth's store. Now here you are — stuck beside some long green fat ugly thing that wiggles in a jar. Well, Herman, you got yourself into this mess with your smiling through the bars, and curling your cute little tail, and wanting a bigger, fancier cage. Well, Herman, what now? Huh, Herman?"

Then Herman thought of something he had tried at Woolworth's when he was unhappy. He had learned to smile at the big fat people faces, and sometimes they even smiled back. "Smile Power," he called it. So now, all alone in

Marc's room, Herman tried smiling at the big fat ugly caterpillar. It did not smile back. At first it only wiggled a bit. But as Herman kept on smiling at it, an amazing thing happened.

The caterpillar slowly climbed up a small branch in the jar. Before long, a wisp of a thread began to appear around the caterpillar. As the thread got longer and longer, the caterpillar wrapped himself in it. Soon Herman could not even see the caterpillar. Herman watched, absolutely amazed. "That," he thought, "is a neat trick. In fact, it is the neatest trick I have ever seen."

Herman tried to do it. Round and round his cage he ran, trying to make any old kind of thread. But the only thing he could make was spit, and at last he had to give up. But he learned an important thing: A MOUSE CANNOT SPIN A COCOON!

Up and Away

A few days later, Marc did not go to
school. He peered into Herman's cage
with a wild, happy look on his face and
told his mouse: "You, Herman, are going
to be an astronaut!" Marc was sort of
pretending when he called Herman that
— but how's a mouse to know?

Marc picked up Herman's cage, carried
it outside, and put it on a big table in a
pretty patio. On the table was a small
plastic bowl and lots of string. Tied to
a chair, and floating above it, were five

14

big beautiful balloons of different colors.

First Marc made holes in a lid that fitted over the small bowl. Then Marc's mother brought out some cotton and Marc put it in the bottom of the bowl. Next Herman was put into the bowl on top of the cotton and the lid secured. The last thing Herman heard was Marc's mother saying, "Maybe he will not like it," and Marc answering, "Oh Mother, of course he'll like it!"

At first Herman did not like it. He could not run or even walk around, and he missed fresh air. Marc was very careful when he tied the string around the plastic bowl and to the balloons, for he did not want to lose his pet. All this time Herman was wondering, "Why did I ever want to leave Woolworth's?"

Oops! Imagine yourself sitting in a bowl on a table and then all of a sudden you start to go up! That's what happened to Herman when Marc tied the balloons onto the string around the bowl.

At first it was only a little bit up, and he was floating a few feet above the table. Then as Marc gradually loosened more and more string. . . up, up, and up went Herman.

He passed the wall of the patio and a bug waved at him from a potted plant. A butterfly circled around his plastic capsule and dipped her wings to him. He could see the branches of a tree, and a nest of baby birds squawking their heads off. They were waiting for their mother to return with food. When the mother Robin flew by Herman, she nearly dropped the worm she was carrying to her family, so surprised she was to see a mouse floating by her.

What a wild, wonderful feeling! Soon all Herman could see were swirling white clouds and the blur of the bright balloons above him.

With his paws Herman parted the cotton in the bowl and looked down through the clear plastic. Once more a neon sign flashed in Herman's brain: YOU ARE BIGGER THAN ANYTHING!

No longer was he just a little mouse. *Everything was smaller than he was!* There was Marc way down there, looking as little as a grasshopper. The patio was as small as his cage. Even the huge cars that had scared him on the way home from Woolworth's — why, they were no bigger than bugs.

For the first time in his life Herman felt big. As he floated up there above the earth he kept saying, "I'm big. . . I'm big. . . I am a GIANT!"

It was dreamy being a giant way up there watching the puffy clouds.

But it did not last long.

The wind came up and began to toss the capsule back and forth. Then Herman did not feel big any longer. He felt green. It was awful. He felt so sick he was sorry to be up in space. Oh, how he longed to come down again — back to the cup of Marc's hands, back to Marc's gentle petting, and back to his own cage. And he never, never wanted to go up again. Herman lay groaning in the bottom of the capsule and squeaked sadly to himself, "I do not want to be an astro-nut!"

Even as sick as he was, somehow Herman knew that Marc really cared for him. If he could just let Marc know how he felt, maybe Marc would understand.

So, just as he had practiced smiling at Woolworth's, Herman practiced something else while he lay groaning up there. Do you have any idea what he practiced?

He remembered what Marc's mother had said just before he went up: "Maybe he will not like it." Herman had under-

stood this, but if only he could say it!
Then he could make Marc understand
how he felt.

As he rolled back and forth, Herman
did not make any old sort of groans. He
tried to groan, "I do not like it." At first
it came out "eeek eeek uhhhheeek." Then
it was "eeeiiii ooooooo ahhhhh eeeee."

But as Herman kept practicing, his
eeeks and his groans began to get closer
and closer to words.

At last he felt a tug on the string.

At last he was being pulled down
again. And he kept on practicing.

As he passed the tree, his "I do not like
it" sounded like "Yeeeiiiii ddcccccoooo
nooooteeee liiiii eeet." Better, but still
not good enough.

As he passed the potted plant, his
sounds became "Iiiiieeee ddooooeeeee
nooooeeee liiiii eet."

Would Marc understand?

Oh, how much better Herman felt when the top of the bowl was taken off and he saw Marc's face above him. He took a deep breath of fresh air. *"Now or never,"* he thought, and said: "Iiee dooee no liiee eet."

Marc's bubble gum dropped out of his mouth.

"What did you say, Herman?"

"Iiiii do not liik eet."

Marc yelled for his mother, who was inside the house. "Mom! Mom! Herman said he doesn't like it! Herman can talk!"

His mother was very busy and she called back, "That's nice, dear."

Marc held Herman very gently in the cup of his hands and told him, "Don't worry, Herman. If you do not like it, you don't ever have to go up into space again! Is that okay?"

Herman smiled. "Ooooee kayee!" he squeaked most happily.

Herman at the Art Show

HERMAN was a lucky mouse to have picked Marc as his boy. Marc liked to take him places. He took Herman to the zoo, to the park, and even to a used-car lot when his mother wanted to pick out a car to buy.

One day Marc told Herman, "Today we are going to an art show. It is about time you got some culture."

"What," asked Herman, "is *kull-choor?* Is it something to eat?" He hoped it was, for he was getting tired of the grain he got everyday.

"No, it is not something you eat," said Marc. "Uh, culture is. . . uh, well, it is a very hard thing to explain. All I know is that it is very important. Art is part of it, and my mother is an artist and she is going to be in a show. I cannot explain art either. You have got to see it to believe it!"

By now Marc knew Herman was not going to run away, so he did not have to carry him in the cage. Herman liked to travel in the pocket of Marc's blue-striped shirt.

One time Marc carried him around in his red-checked shirt and Herman was dizzy for days. Every time he opened his eyes he saw red checks, even when they weren't there. However, blue stripes he found restful but not dull. He could feel safe and snug deep in Marc's pocket or he could peek out the top whenever he wanted to see what was going on.

So Herman went to the art show in the pocket of Marc's shirt. They rode in the front seat of the car. The back seat was full of paintings by Marc's mother.

At the art show, artists were busy putting their paintings into frames and hanging them on the wall just so.

First Marc took Herman on a tour so he could meet the artists and see their paintings. There were paintings of trees, of the sea, of people. Some were just splashes of bright colors. One artist used colored toothpicks and paper clips, which he glued on paper in different designs.

Some of the artists were housewives like Marc's mother. One artist had a woolly beard, green-and-white striped pants, and a fur vest. His paintings were big colored blobs. He took time to explain one of his blobby paintings to Marc, who listened politely.

"The green streak," the artist said, "is my father taking me to the park. This black one is when I fell off the garage roof when I was four, and this purple part is when I got sick on green apples. You see, to me green apples are really purple."

Herman was quite interested in art. He was really a very cultured mouse. His favorite was a great big painting of a huge chunk of yellow cheese. He thought it was the most beautiful thing he had ever seen.

After the tour, Marc sat down at a long table with other children. They were the sons and daughters of the artists. On the table were bright paints in cupcake pans, large pieces of paper, and brushes. As Herman watched from Marc's pocket he saw all the children painting. He wanted to try it too, but the brushes were longer than he was.

Then Herman had a wild idea. Quietly he crept out of Marc's pocket and climbed down Marc's shirt to the table below. Carefully he crept onto a cupcake tin and looked at all the colors. Then ever so gingerly he dipped a paw into some red paint. Then he jumped. He jumped right onto a big piece of paper lying on the table. Before anybody noticed, Herman had made five tiny red paw prints on the paper in the shape of a smile. He was very pleased and he squeaked "Haw" in mouse language, which came out "Hee-hee."

Marc said, "Hey, look at Herman! He's painting!"

By this time Herman had hopped back onto the pan and had dipped another paw into some purple paint. Back onto the paper he leaped, and, while the children laughed, he made a swirly, whirly "S" in purple paw prints.

"My mouse, the artist!" said Marc proudly.

Herman was having a great time at the art show. He enjoyed painting more than anything he had ever done in his life. All that afternoon Herman dipped his paws and his tail into different colors and worked on his design.

With purple he painted his puzzlement at the people who did not like mice. By running in black straight across the paper he painted his quick but unhappy goodbye to his mother, his sisters, and brothers. Green wavy paw prints running zigzag were how sick he felt in outer space. And orange was the fun he felt at this wonderful art show. Herman had never had such a good time.

When he got through, the big paper was full of paw prints in different colors. The children put Herman's painting in a spare frame and propped it up against a wall to see how it would look. They all thought it looked splendid!

All artists have to clean up after they paint. Marc's job was to wash the cupcake tins. This was easy because he had done it many times. But how do you clean up a painted mouse?

Marc came up with a very good idea. He washed one of the cupcake tins and filled it again so that each of the eight cups were full of clear water. Then he told Herman of his plan. Carefully Herman put his strawberry red paw into the first cup. The water was just right — not too cold nor too hot. Marc had been careful about that. Then Herman jumped in and took a bath.

He took eight baths. As soon as the water in one of the cupcake tins became full of paint, Herman jumped into the the next one.

After all of these baths there was still

paint left on Herman's upper back and his nose. Marc filled a small paper cup full of water, told Herman to shut his eyes, and then he kept pouring the water over Herman, a little bit at a time.

It was Herman's first shower bath, and he was not sure he liked it. But he did not want to be red, purple, green, black, brown, orange, and blue all the rest of his life. In the middle of the shower Herman looked like a rainbow mouse, but at last he was squeaky clean, whiter than white — as clean as clean can be. Now they could go home.

Who Did It?

THE next morning Marc put Herman in his pocket to go back to the art show. Herman was still sound asleep — and snoring. If you have ever heard a mouse snore, you know that it sounds like someone whispering "awk-pushew."

When they arrived at the art show, Herman was still "awk-pushewing" deep in Marc's pocket. When he woke up, he heard the judges talking, but he couldn't understand what they were talking about.

Sleepily, Herman peeked out, but all he could see was a big crowd of people. So he yawned and went back into the bottom of Marc's pocket.

Still half asleep, Herman listened and heard one of the judges say, "Now it was most interesting that when it came to first prize, we all agreed for once. Very unusual!" The people politely laughed. "We all agreed because one painting here was so different — a sweeping study of new style! So will the painter who did this fine work come up for her or his prize!"

Herman wanted to see the best painter get his prize, so he sleepily poked his head out again. But once more all he could see was a crowd of people. Marc was curious too, so he began moving to the side of all the people and peeked over the arm of one of the judges.

"Isn't the artist of this fine first-prize

painting here today?" asked the main judge.

Marc's mouth popped open — wide open — with complete surprise. There was Herman's painting — not where the children had left it on the floor — but hanging up on the wall. And the judge was pointing to it.

(What everybody did not know was that during the night, the janitor had come in to clean up. Seeing Herman's painting on the floor he thought it had dropped off the wall by mistake. So he hung it up beside the other paintings.)

By this time the judge was really puzzled, and all the people were muttering. "Does anyone know who painted this picture?" the main judge asked.

Several of the children jumped up and down, pointed to Marc, and said, "Herman! Herman!"

Marc's face got very red. Everybody

was looking at him, and he was afraid they would be very mad when they found that a small white mouse was the winner. How was he going to explain?

"Herman," he whispered, "Herman you come on out!"

Herman did not obey.

Marc found that when he tried to explain, his own voice squeaked. "Uh, Herman," he said, "Herman is my — "

At this point, Herman poked his head up over Marc's pocket, and a lady in the crowd spotted him.

"A MOUSE! A MOUSE! HELP! A MOUSE!" she shrieked, and several other ladies began screaming also.

"Yes," said Marc, bravely. "Herman is a mouse."

Then all the children began to explain how Herman had painted the prize-winning picture. They also explained they had never meant to enter it in the contest.

Everybody was talking and yelling and it was BEDLAM (which means everything was noisy and very mixed up).

Marc felt terrible, but he felt even worse when he saw his mother sitting down with her head in her hands. He knew she had wanted to win a prize, and he thought she was crying. Marc went over to her, put his hand gently on her shoulder and said, "Oh, Mom, I'm sorry!"

"Sorry?" His mother looked up. She was not crying. She was laughing! She was laughing so hard she could hardly talk. "Oh, Marc," she told him, "do you realize you've got the only prize-winning artist mouse in the world?"

Other people had begun to laugh too. Only one man did not laugh — a tall young man with a very angry face. He picked his toothpick and paper clip design off the wall, announced that he was not going to be in any art show for mice, and stomped out.

Nobody seemed to miss the angry artist. Everybody was more interested in Herman. The reporters from the newspapers knew that here was a great story. And they took lots of pictures of Herman with his painting, Herman with Marc, and Herman with his prizes — which were bigger than he was. Herman had won a big purple ribbon and a check for $100.00.

So Herman was not only a prize winner — but he was also a RICH MOUSE!

A Mouse and His Money

NOW that Herman had money, he had a problem: what to do with his money. Most people make money because they need or want certain things. With Herman it was the other way around. First came the money, and now Marc kept asking him, "What do you want, Herman? What do you want, Herman? *Herman, what do you want, huh?*"

Want. Here was a new word, and it was very hard for Herman to get used to it. Up to now he had depended first on his mother or the store, then on Marc. And they had always given him what they thought he should have. Now it was up to him to decide what he wanted to do with his money.

It was a Very Big Step.

It was such a big step that Herman sat thinking about it for hours. Every day Marc would ask things like: "Herman, do you want some bubble gum?" (This was Marc's favorite way of spending his allowance money.) Or, "Herman, do you want baseball cards? Herman, do you want some popcorn? Herman, do you want some bubble gum? Herman, how about a hamburger? Herman, try some bubble gum. Herman, do you want a snow cone? Herman, don't you want some bubble gum, huh?"

Finally, just to make Marc happy, one day Herman did try some bubble gum.

Marc broke a tiny piece off. Herman popped it into his mouth and chewed. Just like Marc told him to do, he chewed very hard.

"This is not fun," thought Herman. "This is very hard work." But he kept on chewing.

At last the gum was ready for blowing. Herman blew. He blew so hard, the wad of bubble gum popped out of his mouth — and landed on Marc's nose. Marc laughed and put another piece in Herman's mouth. "This," thought Herman, "is ri-dic-u-lous!" But Herman chewed some more.

"Blow, Herman, blow now!" ordered Marc.

This time Herman saw a tiny bubble come out.

"Herman, you did it!" Marc shouted. "Keep blowing!"

Herman's checks puffed out. He blew

harder and harder. It was hard work. The bubble got bigger and bigger. Soon it was as big as his head.

"Keep blowing!" yelled Marc.

Now the bubble was as big as Herman.

Then it happened. With a giant POW-WUP, the bubble exploded and blew Herman halfway across the room. Marc thought it was wonderful. Herman thought it was just sticky. But at least he had found out what he did *not* want to spend his money on — bubble gum.

After two weeks Herman still did not know what he wanted, so Marc told him he should put his money in the bank.

"What is a bank?" Herman asked.

Marc told him, "A bank is a place where they will keep your money safe. And when you want to, you can take it out. If it is a good bank, they will also add extra money to it the longer you leave it there. This extra money is called interest."

This sounded like a good deal to Herman, so he told Marc, "Yes, that is what I want. I want to put my money in a bank."

The next Saturday morning, Marc put Herman and his check for $100.00 in his pocket, and rode on his bicycle to the nearest bank. Outside there was a sign that said NO PETS ALLOWED, but Marc did not notice it. He was too excited about getting Herman a bank account. There were other signs inside the bank. At one counter there was a sign, *New Accounts*, and behind the counter two ladies were typing at their desks and a man was talking on the telephone.

Marc and Herman waited for somebody to notice them. Finally Herman got tired of waiting in Marc's pocket, so Marc put him on the counter where Herman stretched and stretched.

Then one of the ladies behind the counter noticed. Her eyes bugged out. She stopped typing and she came over very fast.

"Little boy," she told Marc (with a look at Herman which made him wish he were back in Marc's pocket), "didn't you see the sign outside? *No pets allowed! And especially mice!* Ugh!"

Marc was very brave. He stroked Herman with his finger, so he wouldn't be afraid, and said, "But you don't understand, ma'am. Please. This mouse wants to open up a new account."

The lady did not understand. She got madder and raised her voice. "Young man," she said, "you are very funny, but we do *not* have time for jokes right now. We are *very* busy!"

By now the man behind the counter

was finished talking on the phone. He came over and asked, "Miss Twiddle, is there anything wrong?"

"Oh, Mr. Brown," she said, "I'm sorry you were bothered. This boy here is just playing a joke. He says his mouse wants to open an account with us."

Marc took out Herman's check for $100.00 and showed it to Mr. Brown. "It's true," he said. "My mouse Herman won this money and he has decided he wants to put it in your bank."

"Is this," Mr. Brown asked, "is this *the* Herman, the mouse artist? Why, Miss Twiddle, didn't you see Herman's picture in the paper a few weeks ago?"

Miss Twiddle smiled a rather sickly smile. "No, Mr. Brown, I did not."

"Well, that's all right," said Mr. Brown, as he turned to look at Herman's check. "I'll take care of this customer myself."

But when Mr. Brown looked at the

check he frowned. "Hmm," he said to Marc. "I see the check is not made out to you, but to Herman. That makes it harder. Now, why don't we just put the account in your name, Marc, and then when you need something for Herman you can take out money for him."

"No," said Marc firmly but politely. "Herman earned the money. Herman wants his own account."

"But," Mr. Brown said, "Herman must sign the back of the check to make it good. Can Herman sign his name?"

"No," admitted Marc. "Can I sign for him and then Herman can sign with his paw print?"

Mr. Brown smiled. "That is a good idea," he said, "but before we can do it I will have to get an okay from our head office downtown. Please wait while I telephone."

Mr. Brown was on the telephone for a

long time. The bank had never had a mouse customer before, and nobody knew what to do. Finally he had to talk to the president of the bank.

At last Mr. Brown came back and told Marc, "Yes, it is all set. Fill out this card for Herman and sign his name. Herman can sign the card with his paw print, and we will keep the card in our files. Then Herman must sign the check exactly the same way."

Marc filled out the card. Herman squeaked to Marc that he would like to sign not only with a paw print, but with a tail swish too. So his signature looked like this:

He was very careful to make his signature on the check look the same as his paw print and tail wiggle on the card.

Mr. Brown asked Miss Twiddle for a bank book. It was a clean shiny blue one, and Mr. Brown wrote "Herman" in large letters at the top of the first page. He wrote the date, and next to it he wrote: $100.00.

Herman was *very* proud of his bank book. But it was bigger than he was, and he had a hard time holding on to it.

As they left the bank Marc did see the sign which said NO PETS ALLOWED. "That sign should be changed," Marc told Herman, with a smile. "It should be changed to say, 'No pets allowed — *except those with money!*' "

"Hmm," thought Herman. "People are very strange. Why should having some money make me different or better than all other mice?"

Herman Goes to School

THE next morning, a Sunday, Marc was awakened early by Herman squeaking at him from his cage. Marc had never heard Herman sound so excited.

"I have been thinking — thinking all night," he squeaked, "and there is something else I want. I would like to go to school!"

"School?" mumbled Marc, and the shock of Herman's request woke him up quickly.

"I must go to school so I can learn to write my own name on my checks. And I want to be able to read books and funny papers like you do too!"

"Whew," thought Marc. "A reading-writing-talking-artist mouse with money. How about that?" Marc said out loud: "Herman, if you keep on like this, you won't be my pet much longer!"

However, Marc did not want to hold Herman down. It might be nice to order Herman around and have Herman feeling grateful for small favors, like choice morsels of cheese.

But Marc wanted Herman to be happy. And Marc was wise enough to know that Herman was a mouse who wanted to grow. Not the kind of growth of just getting bigger in size. The "learning" kind of growth. Herman had the kind of mind that wanted to reach out to the entire world and find out as much as he could.

Marc understood. Even though he was a boy who liked baseball and dodge ball, he also liked to read. And he knew that books made him happier and made the world more interesting.

So, on Tuesday, which was the day the children were allowed to take their pets to school, Marc took Herman. At first Herman did not like it. It was worse than Woolworth's store. All the children crowded around and the girls said things like, "He's so cute! Oh, look at him wiggle his nose! Oh, isn't he cute! Oh, ha, ha — he twitched his tail! Oh, isn't he adorable!"

Herman tried to hide. He pushed all the sawdust to a back corner of his cage and buried himself in it. Then all the children laughed. All they could see was a hill of pine shavings wiggling with every breath Herman took and one mouse eye peeking out.

One of the lessons for the day was about poetry. The teacher read the children some funny poems and talked about words that rhyme. She asked one boy what his favorite word was, and when he said *skunk*, the teacher laughed. She said that was a good word — and could the children think up any rhymes for it? The rhymes they thought up made even Herman laugh — *punk, hunk, bunk, trunk*. One boy put them all together.

"There was a punk skunk
came out of a tree trunk,
crawled in my bunk.
Oh boy, how me and my
punk bunk stunk!"

When the children finished giggling at this, the teacher told them that each could make up his own silly poem, and for a while they were very busy writing. Herman came out to watch them because he wanted to learn to write too.

Herman was quite surprised when the children read their poems. Some were about him! One boy had written:

Marc R. had a little mouse
His nose was pink and red.
This little mouse could paint so well
He soon earned lots of bread.

Herman's favorite was written by a quiet little yellow-haired girl:

Herman is so very shy
All he shows us is one eye.
I think this mouse
Needs a house!

A house? Now Herman had never thought about having a house before, but all afternoon at school he *did* think about it. A house to hide in when everybody was staring at him. A house of his very own. After all, hadn't Marc kept asking, "What do you want, Herman?"

So when they got home and Marc asked, "Well, Herman, how did you like school?" Herman answered eagerly, "I liked it. And now I know what else I want. I want a house. A house of my very own!"

Marc was amazed. A house! A mouse house.

"But aren't you happy in your cage?" he asked Herman. After all, the cage had cost Marc $6.50 of his own money.

Now Herman did not want to hurt Marc's feelings, so he told him: "Yes, I like my cage, but I would like a house too! It does not have to be a big house. A little house just my size will do."

"Herman, are you sure you don't want some bubble gum instead?" asked Marc.

"No," Herman said. "I do not want any bubble gum. I would rather have a house. A house of my very own."

A House for a Mouse

THAT afternoon, when Marc went
bicycling with his best friend, John, he
told him what Herman had said about
wanting a house. John thought that was
a great idea. John liked to make things.

"Let's do it!" he told Marc. "Let's make
Herman a far-out house!"

Late that afternoon the two boys
bicycled back to Marc's house.

"First," said John, "we have to find a
box. A box small enough to fit inside the

door of Herman's cage but big enough for Herman."

They hunted all over for such a box. A shoe box was much too big and so was a cereal box. They found a beautiful gold box that had held hair shampoo but it was too skinny for Herman. Then at last they found the perfect box. It had been in the wastepaper basket all this time. It was a box that had held a jar of cold cream, and it was just three inches square. It had writing on it: *For a more exciting, younger you, pat on your face before going to bed.*

"Yuk," thought both Marc and John. They knew Herman wouldn't want a house that said things like that.

"It doesn't matter," said John, "because we can cover the box with crazy things. Do you have any old magazines?"

"Lots," said Marc. "My mother says we have too many magazines."

For at least half an hour both boys snipped and tore out colored bits — and sometimes whole pages — from a big pile of old magazines. It wasn't long before they had enough for six houses. Then the real work began — selecting the best colored pieces for the mouse house.

"I want to do the front!" said John. "I'm going to make it real weird."

"Okay," Marc agreed. "You do the front and the back. I'll do the sides. I'm going to cut a window so Herman will have a view."

It was at least an hour before the mouse house was finished, but it was a masterpiece! On one side it was bright yellow with purple window-shutters. For the back, John had found a red square with a big white heart. The front was best of all. It was black with a red streak, and on the door John had pasted a horrible-looking big eye from an advertisement for mystery books. He had cut a tiny hole in the center of the eye so Herman could peek out without anyone seeing him.

But would Herman like it?

They decided to surprise him. They put the small house on the big dining-room table and took Herman out of his cage.

At first Herman did not see his house. There were other things on the table that he wanted to explore — books, an ashtray he could crawl into, and leftover snips of magazines. When Herman finally did see the little house, he just sat and stared. Then he began to run around it, sniffing all the way. The boys had left the door partly open and were happy when Herman poked it open wider with his nose and walked into his house. It was just his size!

"Is it mine?" he squeaked. John and

Marc laughed. All they could see of Herman was his head peering out the door, and Herman's nose next to the giant eye looked so silly!

"Do you like it?" the boys asked. But Herman was too busy seeing if he could turn around in the house. Suddenly Herman discovered the window. He popped his head out of it and squeaked, "I like it! I like it!"

Over and over Herman kept going in and out of his house, trying out the door and the window. Finally he asked, "Can I put things inside my house?"

Marc told him, "If you put any furniture in your house, there won't be room for you."

"I do not mean furniture," Herman squeaked. "Can I paste things on the walls inside?"

"Like what?" asked Marc, a little dazed.

Herman began looking over the pile

of leftover magazine snips and pages. For the back wall he chose a painting of a beautiful Japanese lady, and for the side wall he chose small Coca-Cola bottles. The third wall he lined with photos of books.

That night he happily slept in his little house and dreamed the Japanese lady was serving him Coca-Cola while he read the books.

Read. Could he — a mere mouse — learn to read and even to write? That really would be Something Better!

Freedom!

THE next time Herman visited school, the teacher asked the children about a word Herman had never heard before. The word was *freedom*.

"What is freedom?" she asked the class. Here is what some of the children said:

"Freedom is when I come from school and I don't have any homework and I can play with my friends."

"Freedom is when I go to the 31 Flavors
Ice Cream place and I can have any
kind of ice cream I want, like peanut
butter or baseball nut."

"Freedom is when you can do just what
you want and nobody says, 'Don't do that!' "

"But what," asked the teacher, "if you
want to throw rocks at somebody? Or
pick somebody's flowers? Or steal something?"

Many children began talking at once,
and they agreed this was a bad sort of
freedom.

"Why?" asked the teacher.

"Because," said one boy, "it is stepping
on somebody else's freedom."

"Very good!" said the teacher. "Now,"
she asked, "is Herman free?"

Herman leaned against the bars of his
cage, amazed at their answers.

"Herman's not free because he's in a
cage."

"Herman can't travel where he feels like going. He has to wait for Marc to take him places."

"Herman's not free because he does not have a car. My mother said in order to be free she has to have a car."

Mostly the children agreed that being in a cage would be terrible — like being in jail. One boy got very excited and said, "If I were Herman, I know what I would do. I would learn how to open the door with my nose and my paws, and I'd slide right out of there!"

The children clapped and cheered, as if the boy were Lincoln reciting the Gettysburg Address.

All of this was most astonishing news to Herman. He had always thought of his cage as being his home. Hadn't Marc bought him the best cage? He had always thought that "Something Better" meant "The Best," but maybe not. Perhaps

"Something Better" also meant Freedom.

This new way of thinking was enough to keep Herman's mouse brain busy for a long time. All day — at school, coming home with Marc, and that afternoon — he thought about it. He even thought about it at dinner, when Marc tucked a bit of choice cheese between the bars of his cage.

"If I were free," thought Herman, "I could have cheese whenever I want!"

That night, after everybody was asleep, Herman decided to make a break for his freedom. It was a big decision for a small mouse to make.

That boy at school had made it sound so easy, but Herman soon learned it wasn't easy. He tried poking his nose between the bars of his cage door and lifting up his head. Nothing happened at first, except he got a very sore nose. But he kept on trying. He stuck his nose even further through the bars and strained with all his mouse might.

Herman was just ready to give up when suddenly he felt the door rise. Oh, not enough to get even one paw through — but Herman felt as if a volcano was about to explode inside of him. He lifted his nose higher and up rose the door a bit more — enough for one paw, then the other, to squeeze through. He was nearly *free!* All he had to do was pull his nose out from between the bars.

But now his nose was stuck between the bars of his cage! He strained and wiggled every which way. An awful thought whirled through his mouse brain: Would he have to stay stuck like this all night?

Herman lay against the bars of his cage, resting his very sore nose. Then he

gritted his teeth, gave a wild jerk —
and at last his nose came free. Luckily
the tips of his paws were still under the
door. It took just a few seconds to lift the
door up a bit more with his paws and to
slide his head through the opening. Now
both paws were on new territory —
Marc's bookcase.

What a strange feeling to hear his
cage door clank behind him.

FREE! He, Herman, was free.

But free to do what? The first thing
Herman found out was: FREEDOM
IS NOT MUCH GOOD UNLESS YOU
KNOW WHAT TO DO WITH IT.

The house was so silent — so different
at night. Suddenly he knew what he
wanted to do first. He would find out
what things looked like at night.

Now, people say that Christopher
Columbus was brave to set forth and
explore an ocean he did not know. But so

was Herman that first night, for remember, he had never explored alone before.

First of all, he pulled himself up on the bedcovers and took a peek at Marc sleeping. Marc was buried under the covers. It looked as though he was in a cave made of blankets.

Next Herman decided on a daring idea. He would explore Marc's chemistry set. He crept over to the chemistry set and sniffed. Phew! How could Marc spend so much time mixing chemicals?

Suddenly Herman heard a strange and terrible noise coming from outside Marc's room. It sounded like the roar of a car's motor followed by the hissing of a windstorm — but it was in the house!

Slowly Herman began creeping down the hall toward the sound.

"Brrrr phew! Brrrr phew!" It sounded like a snorting hungry monster. Herman crept toward the awful noise.

As he got closer he was astonished to find out that the wild sounds were coming from the mouth of Marc's father.

So the second truth Herman learned from his new freedom was: SOME PEOPLE LOOK AND SOUND VERY SILLY WHEN THEY SLEEP!

Now Herman was feeling bolder and he decided to explore downstairs. And what's more, he decided to go down the way Marc often did — by sliding down the bannister. But when he got to the top and looked down, he muttered to himself, "You are one crazy mouse, Herman!" It looked so steep! Then he saw something that spurred him on.

Down below, moonlight was shining on Marc's school books spread out on the living-room table. Herman wanted to explore those books. To him books seemed like the most mysterious and wonderful things in the world. He knew that in a book, smaller than his cage, were information and pictures about places many miles away and stories about people who lived hundreds of years ago.

If only he could read books! He, Herman — a dinky little mouse, smaller than an orange, quieter than a whisper — would learn about the whole wide world. He would be able to find out what was going on someplace else or what had happened a long time ago. He would feel even bigger than the day Marc had put him up in a balloon and he had floated high above the earth.

So, atop the bannister, Herman gritted his small teeth and let go ... oh ... oh ... oooooohhhh!

It was like sledding down a slick ice mountain! His fur stood up on end and halfway ... eeee ... yiiii! There was a big drop coming! When he got to it, he leaped as far as he could — he made it!

He landed on a big pillow just to the left of the stairs. The wind was knocked out of him and he just lay back, seeing stars — real stars for the first time in his mouse life. He had landed in front of a big picture window and was looking out into the night.

Uhmmm. Maybe being free was just lying back and looking at the stars. For a beautiful time Herman basked in the moonlight. At last he was ready to climb up on the table and explore the books.

Imagine trying to turn the pages of a giant book ten times bigger than you are! This was the first trick Herman had to master — rather difficult for a mere mouse. The best way, he soon learned, was to stand just below the right-hand corner of the book, then flick a page with his nose, grab it with his paws, quickly jump on the book, and run with the page until it dropped over on the other side.

Most of all, Herman enjoyed looking at the pictures in Marc's geography book. He was looking for two special pictures which Marc had showed him several weeks before: *The Grand Canyon at Sunset* and *New York City at Night!* When he found them, they still seemed bright and beautiful — even by moonlight. Sitting on the book with the big color pictures in front of him, Herman could even pretend he was really there.

At sunrise, a rather tired but quite proud mouse made his way back to his cage, stopping off to whisper into Marc's ear, "I know what I want to do next. I want to visit the Grand Canyon — and New York City too!" Marc smiled in his sleep.

When he woke, he thought, "What a nutty dream!"

Herman Dreams
the Impossible (?) Dream

OVER and over again Herman was glad he had picked Marc for a master. It's not easy to take books, lunch, and a pet mouse to school on a bicycle every day. But Marc did it.

Also, Marc let Herman ride around the house in a small battery-operated model car. Herman really liked this. Mr. Reed, Marc's dad, boasted "Well, I guess we are now a three-car family!"

Sometimes on weekends, while Marc's

mother was painting, she let Herman use her paints. He ran around making A-B-C's in splendid colors. He copied the letters out of a handwriting book from school. Herman felt that staying alive in the outside world could depend upon his being able to write STOP, SMILE, or LOVE before he got wiped out by some-body who hated mice.

In the evening, Herman liked to watch Marc's father do his homework. Mr. Reed worked for a firm that made model planes. These were not children's toys. They had real motors, and grownups flew them as a hobby.

Marc's dad had a new idea for a model plane. He had been working on it for three years. This plane had a new type of engine, noiseless and nonpolluting. The plane was worked by punching buttons in a funny big machine "the come-pew-tor". (Now, that is spelled c-o-m-p-u-t-e-r, but Herman had still not learned to spell fancy words.) Herman called this "the magic machine." How else could it make the plane fly around the yard, and even around the park five miles away!

One day Mr. Reed gave Herman a ride in the plane. Herman loved it! This kind of flying did not make him sick the way his ride in the balloon had done. The magic machine took care of that. Whenever the wind was too strong and rocked the plane, the machine made the plane change course. Herman just sat and smiled in the plane while it seemed to fly itself. What fun to zoom this way and that, up in the sky, while Marc watched from the ground below and Mr. Reed worked the magic machine in his office.

Most important of all, Herman helped Mr. Reed. He told Mr. Reed how the plane acted with wind and speed changes.

"My mouse, the test pilot!" said Marc proudly.

So many bright images whirled in Herman's tiny brain — school, paints, writing, reading books, and flying the plane. No humdrum mouse life for him!

One day all these many images came together in his brain and formed one great dream. Herman knew what he wanted next — but WOW, it was WILD!

Herman waited until bedtime, and on the way upstairs he quietly squeaked in Marc's ear:

"Now I know what I want, old buddy. I want to fly all the way across the U.S.A. in that plane. Most of all I want to see what the Grand Canyon really looks like, and I want to see all the lights on at night in New York! *That's what I want!*"

It was late. Marc was very tired and he moaned, "Herman, why don't you just go chew on some bubble gum, huh?"

Herman smiled. " 'What d'ya want, Herman' — that's what you said. "What d'ya want,' you kept asking. *Well, this is what I want!*"

Marc sat down on his bed holding Herman gently in his hand. He knew it was time to tell his little mouse the hard facts of life. "Herman," he said *"you cannot always get what you want."*

YOU CANNOT ALWAYS GET WHAT YOU WANT!!! Like a neon sign this bad news flashed in Herman's brain. It was a tough blow for a very spoiled mouse to take.

"But you never know until you try!" he squeaked.

Marc yawned. "Why, oh, why," he thought, "why did I have to pick out this lively mouse? Next time I will get a nice sleepy one." Gently, Marc put Herman back in his cage. And he promised to try to help his pet with this impossible dream.

"Maybe," thought Marc, as he drifted off to sleep, "maybe it isn't Herman's fault. Maybe I gave him too many of those dumb mouse vitamins!"

Let it be said that not only was Marc a very good master, but Marc's father was also a rare person. Mr. Reed had a wide-open mind. And that's what it takes not to get mad or snarly when your son comes to you and tells you that his pet mouse wants to fly your one and only priceless model plane 3,000 miles across the U.S.A.

Mr. Reed was sure Marc must be kidding. He laughed. This hurt Herman no end. His ears and tail drooped. His small mouse brain drooped too. "He's right to laugh," thought Herman. "I have dreamed the impossible dream! I will just crawl back under my pine shavings!"

Mr. Reed's laughter was understandable. This model plane was the most important work he had ever done in his life. All of Mr. Reed's dreams were wrapped up in it. If the model worked, then all of Mr. Reed's good ideas could be used in bigger planes and boats and cars. People all over the world could be transported without noise and without polluting the air. Mr. Reed could even imagine housewives floating quickly, happily, and safely to markets or flying their children to school! If his model worked and was used — this would greatly improve transportation. It also could make the Reeds very rich. Mr. Reed was some dreamer himself!

How could he think of trusting his great invention to a mere mouse?

Marc stopped his dad's laughter by saying: "But if people see Herman flying your plane — wouldn't that help put it over?"

When Mr. Reed went to bed that night, he couldn't fall asleep. At three o'clock in the morning he got up, put on his bathrobe, picked up Herman from Marc's room, and took him down to the kitchen where they shared a snack.

"Herman," Mr. Reed told him as they munched on salami and Swiss cheese, "Herman, I think you can do it! I really bet you can! Even if you don't succeed, maybe by just trying — all the publicity you would get — might just put the plane over. I'm willing to take a chance on you, you crazy mouse."

Mr. Reed cut another slice of salami. "The computer is, I think, ready to carry the plane all the way to New York. But to be sure, I am going to put controls into the plane that you can work — just in case anything goes wrong with the magic machine, as you call it."

"Wow!" thought Herman as he munched and listened.

"Now of course," went on Mr. Reed,

"you'll have to go into flight training, and we'll have to figure out what way you'll take across the U.S.A. But one of the biggest problems is that it will take 75 batteries to get you all the way across the country. And the batteries will have to be waiting for you at all the places where the plane lands. You know, I think that might be a good problem for Marc to work out — don't you?"

A Surprise for Zippy

ONE morning the Zippy Battery Company in Toledo, Ohio, received an unusual letter.

Dear Sir,

I have a pet mouse, Herman, who wants to fly solo across the U.S.A. from Los Angeles to New York in a model plane that needs batteries.

So could you please give me a list of stores across the country near the main roads where Herman can get your batteries?

Also could your salesmen in the stores put the batteries in the plane for Herman? He cannot do this with his paws.

Herman will need at least 75 batteries.

I hope you can help. Herman is going to be a very unhappy mouse if you cannot.

> Sincerely,
> Marc E. Reed

Everybody at the Zippy Battery Company smiled when they read the letter. It was handed all around and even made the busy president smile. They all thought it was a good joke.

But the seven-year-old son of one of the directors asked his father, "How long will it take Herman? When is that mouse going to leave?" When the father told his son that the letter must be a joke, the boy asked, "*What if it is not a joke?*"

What indeed? What if there really was a mouse who wanted to fly? The whole thing was just too silly. But *if* ... if it were just a little bit true . . . why then it might put Zippy in the news. And this kind of news could sell more batteries. Why not find out more?

One month after Marc had written his letter, a Los Angeles salesman for the Zippy Battery Company stood on the front doorstep of Marc's house, ringing the doorbell and feeling very foolish. Merv Beesley was a serious young man who had just joined the company, and he wanted to get ahead. Imagine being told that your first call would be on a pet mouse!

On the other side of the door, Marc and Herman were not prepared for Merv Beesley either. When they had not heard from the Zippy Company right away, Herman thought, "I have dreamed the impossible dream." He gave up, and for two weeks he just lay sleeping under his pine shavings.

As Merv Beesley watched, Marc tried to wake Herman. Whistling, sweet talking — nothing worked until Marc got a piece of Swiss cheese and waved it in front of his mouse's nose. Slowly Herman shook off the pine shavings, and with only one eye half open stumbled across his cage onto Marc's hand. Worse, he even yawned in Merv Beesley's face.

"This is the mouse that wants to fly across the U.S.A.?" thought the salesman.

While Herman was waking up, Marc showed Merv Beesley his mouse's bank book and his painting. Then Marc took him to meet his father who showed the salesman the plane and set the computer for a test flight on the Reed lawn.

As Herman zoomed above them, the salesman shook his head. The whole thing was crazy. *But it just might work.*

After the plane had made a perfect landing right in front of him, Beesley found himself asking, "When do you want to leave?"

They all agreed it would take at least a month before the plane and Herman were ready. Beesley promised he would phone his company and let them know.

Now nobody at the company thought that Herman would really make it all the way. But just the plane taking off with Zippy batteries would put them in the news and help sales. So the company gave their okay. And their okay meant that Zippy would furnish all the batteries free. Merv Beesley would follow Herman on the trip by car down below and act as his ground crew.

Herman was so happy, he began to train night and day.

In Training

HOW that month whizzed by as Herman trained. There were so many things he had to learn!

He had to learn map reading. Marc found all sorts of U.S. maps and Herman studied them. One night Mr. Reed, Merv Beesley, Marc, and Herman looked over all the maps and planned the route Herman should fly.

Herman also worked on his squeak-talking in case he landed where Merv

Beesley was not around to help. His very life might depend on making people understand him. Over and over he practiced squeaking, "Meeeyiii naaaaam isss Huhr — mann. Eeeeyiii aaahm gooooeeng toooo Neeeoow Yohrk!" He also worked on his paw writing. In case of trouble on the trip he might not have paints and paper, so over and over he made the words LOVE and HELP with mouse tracks in sand and earth.

He also learned Morse code. Marc bought Herman a tiny flashlight, which he could work with his paws. Herman and Marc practiced sending messages to each other, at first in a dark room, then from farther away.

Most important was Herman's flight training. He had to get to feel as though the plane was part of him. And he had to test the plane in two ways: by letting the computer take over, and by using controls that Mr. Reed put into the plane for him to work. Mr. Reed hoped the computer would guide the plane all the way. But in case of trouble, Herman would have to fly the plane himself.

At first Herman flew across the Reeds' back lawn. Then he worked on flying from the Reeds' back lawn to the front yard. In a few weeks he was able to fly from the Reed house to a hill in Griffith Park and all over the Hollywood hills, landing on the back lawns and patios of different friends.

One day the phone rang in the Hollywood police station. The policeman listened politely to a screaming lady and told her not to worry. "Humph!" he said to his partner when he hung up. "These kook calls! Some lady said she saw a mouse flying a plane go right by her kitchen window. Can you beat that one?"

But Herman wasn't the only one who

worked to make his dream come true. All the Reeds helped. Marc's mother made Herman a red poncho in case he got cold, and a hat with a brim to keep the sun from his eyes as he flew.

The last week of training flew by. All of a sudden, it seemed to Marc, the big moment had arrived. The Reeds loaded the plane and Merv Beesley's car with all the things Herman would need — mostly his favorite cheeses. Herman also needed a tiny copy of the map. Ordinary-size maps were too big for the plane.

Then — at last they were at the starting point, a grassy hill in Griffith Park. All about them were television cameras and newspeople.

One TV newsman was talking into his microphone:

"Folks, you won't believe this one. This tiny mouse named Herman is going to try the impossible dream. Get this —

a solo flight in a new kind of model
plane from L.A. to New York.
"The plane is noiseless and nonpolluting!
Its path is set by computer — and if
Herman makes it, why, we may all be
driving cars and flying planes — maybe
even boats — this way! The plane,
made by Ernest Reed, will run on
Zippy batteries.

"Most people here to watch the takeoff
don't think he's going to get very far.
But here's Herman's master, Marc E. Reed.
Marc, what do you think?"

Marc, holding Herman close to his
cheek, said softly: "I think he's going to
make it," and Herman smiled happily
back at him. Marc had a hard time,
though, keeping tears back when Herman
nibbled goodbye.

"Good luck, buddy," Marc whispered,
and the TV cameras rolled in close to
show this touching scene.

Marc put Herman into the plane, and

his mouse waved a paw for the TV cameras. "Goooodddbyyyeee!" he squeaked. Then up — up — and away he went, with Merv Beesley following in his car below.

That night the Reeds sat spellbound at their TV set turning to the news on all the stations to watch themselves. They even let Marc stay up for the eleven o'clock news — luckily. This is what he heard:

"Folks, in answer to all your phone calls, we have this news. Herman, the flying mouse, has made his first landing.
The computer landed him right on the spot where Merv Beesley was waiting with Zippy batteries. *This is wild!* I repeat, Herman is alive and well tonight — in Cucamonga!"

Big Trouble

WHEN Herman was seen on the newscast, the phone lines of newspapers and TV stations were flooded with calls. All wanted to know more about Herman. Many people didn't think the story was true. People even began arguing about it. Some felt that Herman really had squeaked "Goodbyeee" when the plane took off. Other TV watchers said this was impossible. Men could go to the moon — but a talking, flying mouse?

All this time, there was Herman, gliding blissfully up above, unaware that he was causing a great big fuss down below. The computer flew the plane perfectly. Herman was free to watch the glory of the ever-changing land spread out below him. His dream had become real — and it was so good, he felt he must be dreaming!

At last Herman knew why he had wanted to leave the store of his birth. Here was the Something Better he had dreamed about — the big wide beautiful world out there!

HERMAN SAYS U.S.A.
A GIANT ART SHOW
FLYING MOUSE REALLY TALKS!!

After Herman's second landing that's what the newspaper headlines said. The TV stations even showed tiny drawings Herman had made of the land from the air. They looked very nice on color TV.

When Herman came down for his second landing, the newsmen asked him again, "What did you see up there?" Herman had a tough answer ready. You know what Herman said? "A mess!" That's what he said.

As he was gliding above the highway that day, he had seen miles and miles of ugly trash below — trash that people had thrown out of their cars as they rushed through the desert.

When some teenagers heard what Herman said, they got together and went out to the desert to clean up the mess. **HERMAN FIGHTS POLLUTION** said the headlines.

"Mouse Power. That's what my pet has!" said Marc proudly, as the Reeds watched the cleanup party on TV.

And Herman glided happily on.

It was over the Grand Canyon that Herman flew into terrible trouble. As the

Canyon loomed up closer and closer below, it looked like a giant mouth in the center of the yellow desert — two big red lips waiting to swallow him. And that's what it began to do! A sudden, strong windstorm was raging over the jagged cliffs, and a terrible battle began for control of the tiny plane — a battle between the wind and the computer.

Herman could feel the wind pulling him away from his landing site. A terrible thought flashed across his mouse brain: *The wind was stronger than the magic machine!* It was up to him to take over the controls. He must land the plane himself amid these jagged cliffs. And he must land it right away because his battery power was very low!

Herman gritted his small teeth and tried to bring the plane up above the wind. It was too late! The big mouth of the canyon was sucking him in. The wind began tossing the little plane from cliff to cliff. All Herman could do was to steer away whenever a cliff loomed in front of him. Wild flashes of red, of purple, of yellow came at him as Herman rode the windstorm. The plane drifted down . . . down . . . down!

In vain the newspeople and Merv Beesley waited for Herman to land up above the great canyon on the south rim. As the sun sank that evening, many hearts in the U.S.A. sank too. Poor Marc was waiting by the TV set, hoping to hear his pet had landed safely. Herman had wanted to see the Grand Canyon so badly!

Marc went to bed that night trying not to see his little mouse lying alone, cold or hurt on some lonely cliff — and with his father's rare plane smashed. Marc lay awake in the dark asking, "Herman, old buddy, where are you?"

The People of the
Blue-Green Water

WHEN Herman came to, he was lying under a bush. It was late evening and there was not a sign of the plane. Had he cracked it up? When he was strong enough to explore, it seemed to Herman that he had landed in a different world.

It was a land of sparkling blue-green pools and waterfalls. A land where the people had brown, plump, sweet faces and dark eyes. A land where there were no cars, no roads. The main street was a dirt path where the teenage boys raced their ponies.

The plump brown people lived in small homes of wood, stone, and sheet metal. Some homes had only one room, and Herman did not see a TV set, a newspaper, or even a telephone! There was no way to let Marc know he was all right. And these people without TV and newspapers had no idea he was Herman, the famous flying mouse.

Herman had landed in the land of the Havasupai — which means People of the Blue-Green Water. At first Herman, in a daze, thought he had landed in some other country. In truth he was still in the United States. He was among the Havasupai Indians, who have lived at the bottom of the Grand Canyon for hundreds of years.

Herman had landed in the only place

in the U.S.A. where the mail is delivered by burro three times a week.

Herman was really alarmed when he heard the plump brown people talking. They spoke strange words — not English! All of his studying would do him no good. Here he was — hungry. But how could he ask for food? Would he, Herman — the famous flying artist mouse — be forced to steal to keep alive? *To steal!* And Marc had taught him that honesty was the best policy!

Of course Herman was a very unusual mouse, but he was really not so smart as he thought he was. He heard the Indians speaking their own language among themselves. But he did not know that they also speak English.

Luckily for Herman, he did not have to steal. That first evening he found many of the people cooking and eating out of doors in front of their small houses. Herman hid behind a cottonwood tree until the families finished eating. Then he sneaked around, picking up this and that. Mostly he got tiny bits of thick bread. That's all that was left in the dust.

The second day, well fed with scraps he had saved, Herman just watched the people. He knew he might be spending the rest of his life with them. He had better learn how they lived and some of their words so he could talk to them.

In the morning Herman watched the children playing and laughing in a large bright pool of water. The pool was formed from a sparkling waterfall that poured from the walls of the canyon. Herman had always felt he had to be on the go — that he had to keep busy, busy. Now he was happy just to sit in the reeds and watch the sunlight on the water. As the sun moved across the sky, it changed the colors of the pool into many shades of blue and green.

In the afternoon Herman listened to the men and women chatting together as they sat on a bench outside the town store. He watched ladies sitting outside their homes making beautiful baskets.

In the early evening he sat behind a tree while teenage boys raced their ponies past him.

The people seemed to use one word the most. The word was *hanega*. The children said it as they splashed in the sparkling water. "*Hanega*," they said as they sipped on soda pop. When a lady finished a basket, she said it again. A teenage boy said it the loudest. "*Hanega!*" he yelled after he had won a race.

Herman thought that *hanega* meant good. And he was right.

So on the second day Herman wrote HANEGA everywhere. He wrote it with his paws in the pink sand beside the pools. He made it with bits of leftover reeds and bread near the houses and the store. Of course he was seen, but he had to take that chance. He was chased and swatted at, and the children tried to catch him. That evening the people were all talking about him. "Who," they wondered, "is that pesky mouse in the red poncho?" But they were sure that it must have been the children who wrote *hanega* everywhere.

The third day was terrible for Herman. Now even the dogs began chasing him. Wherever he tried to hide, they seemed to find him. At last, worn out and tired, he climbed into an empty basket on a high shelf. Now that the dogs were after him, Herman did not know if he could survive much longer!

In the outside world the headlines told a sad story: **SEARCH ON FOR**

FAMED MOUSE . . . NOT A TRACE OF HERMAN OR PLANE . . . HOPE DIMS FOR HERMAN.

Nobody knew it then, but help was on its way. The next morning, Charley Black, a young Havasupai, came down the narrow trail on his horse. He lived up on top of the Canyon and he was coming to the village to visit his parents. In his pack he carried newspapers about Herman. Now the lovely people of the Blue-Green Water knew who Herman was! But how could they bring him out of hiding?

They spread out all the newspapers with pictures of Marc looking sad on the front page. They put out food, and then they all called in English, "Come out, little mouse! We know who you are, little Herman. Come out, little mouse that can talk. We will not hurt you."

Herman woke to their chanting, and

when he crept shyly out, he was gently picked up by kind hands. All the Havasupai were trying to talk to him at one time. The minute Herman found out that the Havasupai did have one telephone, he made a phone call. And you know who Herman called, don't you?

Then the Havasupai began a great search for the missing plane. And soon they found it! It was covered by a pile of dirt at the side of the road. Herman had put it down safely with only a dent in its side. That was really big news for the outside world!

Now Herman could go on with his trip across the U.S.A. The newspeople wanted to send a helicopter down to the village to pick up Herman and his plane and bring them to the top of the Canyon where Herman could take off. But Herman's new friends, the Havasupai teen-age boys, had a better idea. They would hold a race with their ponies, and the winner would have the honor of bringing Herman up the trail by horseback.

Herman liked the idea. "Oooee-kayee!" he squeaked happily. Herman had learned that one way the Indians earned money was by bringing visiting tourists up and down the trail. And Herman wanted to help them. Besides, thought Herman, what better way is there to see the glory of the Grand Canyon than by peeking out of an Indian boy's knapsack as you ride the trail up and up at sunrise?

The trip was even better than he had dreamed it would be! What peace! What splendid beauty — colors of the cliffs changing at every turn!

As they neared the top, Herman could hear shouting and cheering. A big crowd was waiting — TV cameras, newspaper people, and many fans. It seemed as if everyone in the U.S.A. was waiting for Herman to go on with his trip.

One of the first questions asked by

newspeople was: "Herman, are you going to try to make up for lost time?"

Herman had already talked to Mr. Reed about this on the phone. He stood with his red poncho flapping in the wind and squeaked his answer: No! Now he wanted to take even *more time* to see the U.S.A. Here was another big news story!

Herman said he wanted to see and really enjoy all the different wonders of the land. Then he said that the best kind of seeing was not just seeking out and enjoying what was good. It was also seeing what was wrong and trying to change it for the better.

"Wow!" yelled Marc as he watched his pet on color TV. "That's my mouse that said that!"

But the best part was when Herman introduced his teenage Indian guide, Joe Strongarm. Joe spoke in both English and Havasupai, inviting people to visit his tribe. Joe looked elegant on his pony!

Herman closed the conference by saying that his stay with the Havasupai people and getting to know them was one of the best parts about the trip so far. The TV camera came in for a closeup of Herman perched on Joe's hand. "I want," said Herman, "to get to know other people as I go across the U.S.A."

TV stations all over the country were soon jammed with calls from people who wanted Herman as a house guest!

This meant more work for Mr. Reed. He had to reset the computer in his house every time Herman stopped to visit someone. "It seems," Mr. Reed said to Marc, "that your mouse has his own ideas! Pretty good ones too!"

On with the Dream

SALES of Zippy batteries were soaring and letters came pouring in. Zippy hired a girl to read Herman's mail. Merv Beesley was too busy. He had to rush out and buy more shirts for himself and more cheese for Herman.

It was also up to Beesley to call Zippy each day to keep track of all the people asking Herman to stay with them. There were so many that sometimes it was hard for Herman to choose. It was up to

Beesley to work with people of the press and with Herman's fans. Everyone wanted to know when and where he was landing. Beesley still had to follow below in his car.

"And I thought this mouse would give up the first day!" Beesley said to himself.

Herman, when he flew, could soar above all the fuss below. The hookup was working fine between the plane and the computer in the Reed house. Herman liked to paint the land below as the plane flew.

Everybody in the U.S.A. was following Herman's trip. Children cut out and kept photos and news stories of this brave mouse: Herman at the Petrified Forest, Herman with Cowboys, Herman at the Painted Desert.

Herman never forgot his first friends, the People of the Blue-Green Water. And he taught his fans a new word he had learned from the Indians. "*Hanega*," said Herman, standing in the red earth of Oklahoma. "*Hanega*," he said, as he was photographed in a field of golden grain in Missouri.

Everybody in the U.S.A. began to use this word meaning "good." "*Hanega*," said a little girl in Utah when she saw birds flying. "*Hanega!*" yelled a boy in Maine as he rode his bike.

One newspaperman did a whole story on *hanega*. "Herman," he wrote, "has showed us that we can always try to make things better in the U.S.A. — but we must also not forget to see and enjoy the good. Herman, you are *hanega!*"

In Ohio, Herman got a phone call. It was a long distance call from his Indian friend, Joe Strongarm. Joe was laughing and kidding him. "Is this Hanega Herman?" Joe said. "Hey, I can call you because thanks to you, I'm rich now. All of us in the tribe now are better off. Herman, you got us so much news, we have more visitors than we can take care of!"

As Herman flew closer to New York the headlines counted off the days.

HERMAN SPENDS NIGHT AT PENN-SYLVANIA FARM — WILL BE IN NEW YORK IN TWO DAYS.
HERMAN IN NEW YORK TOMOR-ROW ... MAYOR TO GREET HIM.

From the beginning it had been planned that the best spot for Herman's landing in New York would be Central Park. Also, Herman would have to fly the plane into the city and land it himself, without the help of the computer. Mr. Reed could not manage the landing by computer because of all the tall buildings. Herman had looked at many maps which showed Central Park as a big green space in the center of the city.

Twenty miles away from the city, the computer clicked the controls over to Herman. Oh, but he was happy — and scared too! Below he saw wide roads with cars rushing, rushing like mad, brightly colored beetles. In the distance he could see the tall towers. Some were of glass and were lit up by the afternoon sun.

Soon there was no time to be scared. Herman was too busy steering the plane among all the towers. It was tricky. What made it harder was that the people were at the windows, yelling and pointing. Worse, they began to throw confetti to celebrate, and he had to steer through a blizzard of paper. Children and grownups were leaning out of windows as he passed, screaming. "There he is!" "It's really him!" "Isn't he darling?" "Herman, here I am! Wave a paw." "Look at me, Herman!"

Herman was looking for the park. Where, oh where was it? At last he reached an open space away from the buildings and looked down. And there it was! Filled with people! *Everyone was looking up at him!*

The plane floated lower and lower, and Herman could see police holding back the crowds. Why, there were even signs.

HERMAN FAN CLUB
HERMAN, WE LOVE YOU!

Everyone was screaming.

"Herman," he said to himself, "who is going to save you from all this crazy love?"

Now the plane was at treetop level and he could see a wonderful surprise. There to greet him, standing in the center of a small grassy spot, was MARC!! An airline had flown Marc to New York City for this big moment.

When Herman landed, the people screamed, and the mayor made a speech. All that time Herman just looked into the dear eyes of his beloved Marc. Marc had even worn his old striped shirt — the one that Herman liked best. After the wild greetings it felt good to crawl into Marc's pocket again.

Marc held open the pocket and peeked proudly down at the tired hero. "Hi, old buddy," he said softly. "You made it! I knew you would. But before you go to sleep, guess what? Tomorrow we both have to be on a TV program. Herman, it's going to be a whole hour program, all about you! How about that?"

"Awk-pushew!" snored Herman.

The Herman Spectacular

HERMAN was glad to hide out in Marc's pocket when they arrived at the TV station. It was noisy, and everybody was running about. Most TV shows spend days rehearsing. But the TV director told Marc, "Only four hours rehearsal. Then we tape it. Everybody is waiting for this!"

Three men were in charge of lighting. They had never lit a mouse before. Marc had to stand holding Herman up while they tried bright lights, low lights, and lights of different colors. But Marc kept his sense of humor. "Just color me blue," he whispered to Herman. "What color do you want to be?"

"How about puce?" squeaked Herman, "with purple polka dots!"

A very fussy man and a lady were in charge of scenery. There were a number of sets, based on Herman's life. It was interesting to see how they had done it. What looked like one set was really made up of different parts on wheels that fitted together.

But the TV people had never made a set for a tiny mouse before. They weren't sure at all about the opening set. This was a color photo of a cat with its mouth open. And there was a window, right in the center of the cat's open mouth, where Herman was to peek through. However, after seeing Herman in the cat set they were afraid it looked so real that many children would think Herman was being eaten alive in front of them.

They had not been able to find a mouse stand-in, so Herman had to sit perched in the cat's mouth all the time they were arguing. He got very tired. At last the TV director decided the scene was so scary because Herman looked unhappy.

"Smile, Herman," said the director. "Look alive! Say something!"

"Hee. . . hee. . . heee," Herman squeak-talked. "This is Herman, squeaking to you right from the cat's mouth. Don't be afraid, kids. I'm just hiding out here to get some peace and quiet. No one would think of looking for me here. Besides — who's afraid of the big bad cat?"

"Herman, that's great!" said the TV director. "We'll have you say that when we tape the show, and we'll have the chorus sing "Who's Afraid of the Big Bad Cat?"

The other sets showed scenes from Herman's life. There was one set with fish — the first thing Herman had seen looking out of his cage at Woolworth's. This set included a big fish tank on wheels. Herman noted sadly that he didn't see any of his old fish friends. These were all New York fish, of course.

There was also a group of actors, imitating the people faces at Woolworth's staring and talking about him.

Next they rehearsed the part of Herman's life when he had won the art prize. Several men wheeled in big boards, which fitted together, and these were covered with paintings. Herman saw with surprise that his painting was right in the middle. The network had flown it out from Los Angeles just for the show. There was also a school scene — to show how Herman had learned to read.

Then they rehearsed Herman's flight across the U.S.A. The scene they had the most trouble with was the Grand Canyon. There was a big backdrop with red mountains on it. Then the prop boys wheeled in nine or ten other mountains. They were trying to get the effect of very brightly colored cliffs stretching to the horizon.

"Doesn't it look just like the Grand Canyon?" said the art director proudly. Herman wanted to be polite, but he also had to be honest.

"No," he squeaked.

"Well, of course," said the art director, "I have never seen the Grand Canyon, but it looks just like the pictures of it. Now Herman, I'm going to put you way up here on this platform where you can look down. *Now* doesn't it look just like the Grand Canyon?"

"No," squeaked Herman again, politely but firmly.

The art director was *very* unhappy and so was the director. Even with all the camera tricks, it was very plain the whole thing was phony.

"The trouble is," Herman squeaked to Marc, "nobody can make a Grand Canyon. It's just too much!" Then Herman gently said to the art director, "You really ought to see the real Grand Canyon sometime."

"I'm a very busy man!" the art director said. "I don't have time for that!"

Then the producer's voice boomed out from the control booth. "We're going to cut the Grand Canyon scene. We'll fill in by dragging out the *Surprise for Herman* part at the end."

"*Surprise for Herman?* What's that?" Herman whispered to Marc.

"What's that?" Marc asked the stage director, who smiled knowingly at them.

"Hah — I can't tell you," the director

answered, "because if I told you then it wouldn't be a surprise, would it?"

"Oh, my word," thought Herman. "What are they going to do?" Herman did not want any more surprises. He had experienced enough surprises for one day.

Herman and Marc went to makeup next, and there were more problems. The color white does not look right on TV, and Herman was a white mouse.

Marc had been told not to wear a white shirt for the TV program, but what were they going to do about Herman's whiteness? Back and forth the makeup people discussed this as if Herman were not there.

"We'll simply have to dye him," said the lady in charge of makeup. "We'll dye him pink."

"Not my fur you won't," thought Herman. And he squeaked unhappily in Marc's ear, "Please don't let them!"

"Oh, it won't last forever," he was told. "Just a week or two or maybe three."

"Oh my word," thought Herman, "I do not want to be pink for three weeks. I don't want to be pink for even a day. I do not think I want to be on this TV show!"

At this moment the makeup lady spotted a big box of rosy powder on the dressing table of the makeup room.

"I know the very thing! We will *powder* him pink!

So, while the lady kept patting *Flaming Desire* powder on him with a big powder puff, Herman sat holding his nose. The powder smelled sicky-sweet. All this time he worried about the surprise awaiting him at the end of the show. Marc tried to help his mouse keep a sense of humor during this difficult moment. He told Herman: "The least they could have done was to have the powder perfumed with something you like — limburger cheese!"

"Maybe that's the surprise," thought Herman. "Maybe they're going to present me with a lifetime supply of cheese. Wouldn't that be nice?"

Even at dress rehearsal Herman did not learn about the surprise, but there was no time to worry about it. He had to practice squeak-talking his lines over and over, so the TV viewers would understand him.

Right before the final taping — perched in the cat's mouth for the third time — he was still practicing his lines. Then somebody said, "This is it!" and another person yelled, "Quiet!"

There was a big musical fanfare, and the announcer said, "THE . . . HERMAN . . . SPEC — TAC — U — LAR!"

Herman was very glad he had learned to read. A young man stood in front of him holding up cards with his lines written on them, and this kept him from making mistakes.

After the scenes of his life, the announcer presented many guests. The mayor of the city made a speech. He said he was sorry he couldn't give Herman a key to the city, as he did with most important guests to New York. But the key was bigger than Herman — and Herman didn't need a key. If there really were a keyhole, Herman could climb right through it. Besides, Herman had already climbed into the hearts of all New Yorkers. So said the mayor.

Next came the president of Woolworth's. He reported that his stores across the country had been flooded with calls from children and even grownups — all wanting a white mouse of their own. Because of this, all the mice departments of Woolworth stores would be enlarged.

Not only would more mice be on sale, but also more items for them too. For instance, there would be toys for mice and music for mice so they wouldn't get bored in their cages.

Herman's favorite part came next. The United Nation's Children's Choir gathered around him, and while he sat perched on the hand of a pretty five-year-old girl from India, they sang "Getting to Know You."

Last came a blaring whoop-de-doo of drums and trumpets and the announcer was saying: "Now for the big surprise of the evening . . . a surprise not only for you viewers, but a surprise for Herman too!"

At that moment every light on the stage was turned on him, and Herman could hardly see.

"Presenting . . ." continued the announcer — and there followed another drum and trumpet fanfare — "... presenting the most important guests of *The Herman Spec-tac-u-lar!*"

One of the lights turned to the side of the curtain. Herman was still blinking from the lights, and all he could see was a giant star and two moons in front of him.

Then out of the star came a dear, familiar figure. At first Herman was sure he must be dreaming.

Mother?

In a moment her paws were around him, and she was squeaking, "Herman, your ears are dirty!"

Mother it was. Herman was astonished. Herman was overcome. The TV producer was delighted. "Guh-reat!" he said up in the control booth. "This is the best bit yet." He ordered one camera to come even closer to capture this TV first — the one and only mouse reunion ever to be presented on television.

All day long Herman had been hearing how wonderful he was, and this only embarrassed him. But oh, it felt good to have his mother's familiar paws around him. It was funny, Herman thought, that his mother was still telling him what to do — even after he had soloed across the U.S.A!

Then he saw there were even more surprises. His brothers and sisters had come out behind his mother and were chasing their tails in excitement. Herman was so happy he joined this tail-chasing party. In the control booth the TV director ordered the cameras to pull back to get all the cavorting mice in the TV picture.

Herman was so excited he did not even hear a speech they ran at the end of his show. Even if he had heard it, he wouldn't have believed it. It was a message from the President of the United

States. It had been taped in the White House earlier. The President said:

"My Fellow Citizens: Tonight we are honoring an amazing mouse and his master. Marc and Herman, you have set a wonderful example of what is possible if we humans and animals can work together and help each other make this planet a better place for all. Herman, we are proud of you! You have brought the whole U.S.A. together — watching and hoping you would make it — and we all have enjoyed hearing about the interesting and very different friends you have made across our land."

[Now the President smiled.] "Herman, I don't know what your plans are now, but I hope you don't want to run for President. You are so loved by all the people that I don't think I could beat you!"

Everybody laughed, clapped, and cheered! Then the cameras drew back for a long shot. There was the image of the President smiling on the wall, while underneath him a lot of happy mice were running around Marc.

The Herman Spec-tac-u-lar was over!

The End?

LATE that night, when they got back to the hotel room, there were many messages waiting for the Reeds and for Herman. Some were from companies wanting to buy Mr. Reed's engine. Another man wanted to publish a book of Herman's drawings of the U.S.A. Teachers wanted Marc and Herman to visit their schools. A pet magazine wanted to do a cover on Herman. Merv Beesley called to say that Zippy had given him a better job with more money.

Herman just wanted to crawl into Marc's pocket and sleep. Mr. Reed said, "You are now paying the price of fame, Herman!"

Just before they went to bed, Herman and Marc looked out the window at all the lighted skyscrapers. It looked like a canyon of bright jewels. But for Herman, the best part was that he was seeing it with his tail curled around Marc's finger.

"There it is, Herman," Marc told him. "You saw a picture of New York at night in my book six months ago. You said you wanted to see it for real. Here's your dream come true. How do you like it?"

The little mouse thought of all the people he had seen and all the rushing about he had done in just one day. He was so tired he could not even squeak right and went back to his earliest mouse-squeaking. "Eet's ah nee-ice plaas ta veeseet but eeiii doonoteee leeiik ta leev heer!"

Marc laughed. "Well, whaddya want now, Herman? Huh? Huh? Huh?"

Herman looked sleepily into his beloved friend's eyes and smiled. "Eeeeiiii theeenk iiii want — " he yawned.

"To get some sleep?" said Marc.

"Yesss!" Herman yawned again. Then he looked out the window again at all the lights. "And then — " He smiled at Marc. "Iiii waannt ta seee the holl wiiideee wuurld!"

"What?" Marc groaned. "Oh, good grief, Herman, why don't you just have some bubble gum instead!"